Secret Kingdom
Unicorn Valley

ISBN 978-0-545-53554-0

12 11 10 9 8 7 6 5 4 3 2 14 15 16 17 18 19/0

Printed in the U.S.A. 40
First Scholastic printing, February 2014

Secret Kingdom

Unicorn Valley

ROSIE BANKS

Scholastic Inc.

Contents

A New Adventure

"There!" said Ellie Macdonald, standing back to admire the pretty shapes laid out on the baking tray.

It was a rainy Sunday afternoon and her best friends, Summer Hammond and Jasmine Smith, had come over to bake cookies. Summer had designed hers in the shape of hearts, while Jasmine had made crowns. Artistic Ellie had created cookie fairies.

"How long do we bake them for?" asked Summer, twirling one of her blond braids thoughtfully. "I don't want them to burn!"

"Fifteen minutes," said Ellie, consulting the cookbook.

"Fifteen minutes!" wailed Jasmine dramatically, slumping down in her chair so that her glossy black hair flew around her face. "But I'm starving!"

"It'll go by in a flash." Ellie giggled. "I'll get the timer."

She jumped up from the table where they had been working, then stumbled as she caught her foot on the leg of her chair.

"Oops," she said as it clattered to the floor.

Mrs. Macdonald came in to see what

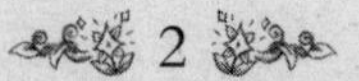

the noise was. "Don't you worry, girls," she said, admiring the cookies. "I'll put these in to bake, and call you when they're done. I'm sure they'll be delicious. And you've made such lovely shapes! Crowns and hearts and even fairies. What imaginations you all have."

While Mrs. Macdonald was putting the cookies into the oven, the three friends exchanged a grin. Of course Ellie's mom thought they had good imaginations — she hadn't been to the Secret Kingdom, the magical land where only a few days ago the girls had actually met a real king wearing a real crown, seen fairies, and eaten magical heart-shaped endless cookies at King Merry's birthday party!

"Let's go upstairs while the cookies are baking," suggested Jasmine loudly. "And check on the Magic Box," she added quietly as the girls headed up to Ellie's room. "Just in case! You did bring it, didn't you, Summer?"

"Of course," Summer said with a smile.

Ellie's bedroom was long and light, with her art books and tools scattered across a big desk and the colorful pictures she'd painted pinned all over the lilac walls.

The girls settled down on the big window seat where Ellie did her painting. Summer carefully pulled the Magic Box out of her bag and passed it to Jasmine, who stared eagerly at its mirrored lid.

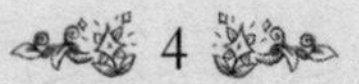

The box was just as beautiful as when they had first found it. Its wooden sides were delicately carved with images of magical creatures, and its curved lid had a mirror surrounded by six glittering green stones.

"It was so lucky we found this at the school rummage sale." Summer smiled.

"We didn't find it — it found us!" Jasmine reminded her. "The Magic Box knew we were the only ones who could help the Secret Kingdom."

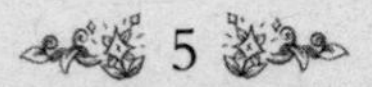

The Secret Kingdom was an amazing place where lots of magical creatures lived — but it had a big problem. Ever since its subjects had chosen King Merry to rule instead of his nasty sister, Queen Malice, Malice had been determined to make everyone in the kingdom as miserable as she was. She'd scattered six horrible thunderbolts around the land, and each of them contained a spell to cause lots of trouble.

"The kingdom still needs our help, though," said Ellie. "We stopped Queen Malice's first thunderbolt from wrecking King Merry's birthday party, but we've only found one of the thunderbolts she hid. Trixibelle said there were six."

"I hope we see Trixi again soon," said

Summer. "It was so wonderful meeting a real pixie."

"Well, it doesn't look like we'll be seeing her today," said Jasmine sadly, putting the Magic Box down and flopping onto Ellie's homemade rag rug. "The mirror's blank."

"No, it isn't!" exclaimed Ellie, grabbing the box and leaning over it. "Look!"

The mirror was starting to glimmer and shine. Words began to float up from its shimmering depths.

"It's a riddle!" said Ellie. She read the words in the mirror out loud:

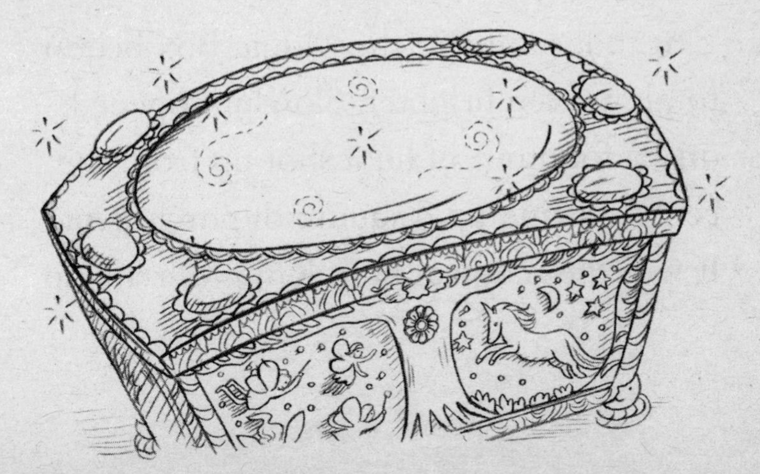

"The second thunderbolt is found
Where one-horned creatures
Walk the ground.
Its wicked magic must be foiled
Before a special game is spoiled!"

Ellie crinkled her forehead thoughtfully. "Creatures with one horn," she said. "I don't know about you, but that makes me think of . . ."

"Unicorns!" broke in Summer, her eyes shining. "There were unicorns at King Merry's birthday party! But I don't know where they live."

At that moment, the Magic Box began to glow even brighter. Slowly it opened, and a fountain of light shot up from the center, lifting up a square of parchment. It was the magical map King Merry had given them after their last adventure! Jasmine unfolded it carefully. It showed the crescent moon–shaped island of the Secret Kingdom. All three girls crowded around the map.

"There's King Merry's palace," Jasmine said, pointing to the pink building with its four golden turrets. The flags at the top of the turrets waved slightly, as if in a breeze.

Summer was looking around the rest of the map. "Flower Forest," she read out. "Dolphin Bay."

"What's that?" asked Jasmine, pointing to a wooded area surrounded by steep hills.

Ellie looked closer. "Unicorn Valley!" she exclaimed. "That must be where the next thunderbolt is!"

They all looked at the Magic Box, but nothing happened.

"What did we do before?" Summer wondered aloud.

"We put our hands on the jewels, then Trixi and King Merry appeared!" Jasmine

remembered. The Magic Box started to glow again, and the friends rushed to press their palms onto the brilliant jewels.

"The answer to the riddle is Unicorn Valley!" Ellie whispered.

For a moment the light coming from the box flashed so brightly they had to shut their eyes. Then it died away, and everything was still.

The girls looked around cautiously.

"Do you think it worked?" asked Jasmine. "King Merry and Trixi appeared in Summer's wardrobe last time."

All three of them looked toward Ellie's wardrobe. Then, behind them, the lid of Ellie's toy chest started to rattle. . . .

Ellie saw it out of the corner of her eye and turned around so fast she almost fell

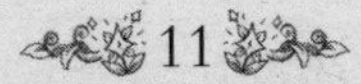

over. "They're stuck in the toy chest!" she cried.

"Don't worry," came a tinkly little voice from among the toys. "I'll be with you in a moment."

"Trixi!" the girls cried happily, recognizing the voice of King Merry's royal pixie, who had guided them around the Secret Kingdom during their last visit.

As they watched, pink petals began to creep around the edge of the lid of the chest. The flowers were growing magically fast, forcing it apart. The lid

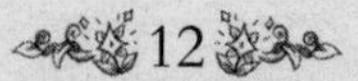

burst open with a shower of petals and Trixi shot out, riding on a leaf. The tiny pixie waved at the girls excitedly, then tapped the magical ring she always wore. It sparkled and the magic flowers dissolved into glittery dust that settled on Ellie's floor before gradually fading away.

Then Trixi floated over to where the girls were standing. "It's lovely to see you again." She smiled, flying her leaf over to each of them in turn and kissing them on the nose.

"You, too," said Summer happily. After their last adventure it had hardly seemed real that they had made friends with a pixie, but here she was, looking just the same — her clothes made out of leaves, her messy blond hair peeking out from under her flower hat.

Trixi's blue eyes twinkled as she smiled at them all.

"But where's King Merry?" Jasmine asked.

"He's busy writing a speech," Trixi told her. "Every year the unicorns hold an event called the Golden Games and King Merry gives a welcome speech to everyone there. Except last time he got confused and arrived at the end of the games, so I had to turn it into a good-bye speech instead!"

The girls all giggled. It was so nice to hear about the Secret Kingdom. But it was even better to go there and have adventures themselves!

"Poor King Merry." Jasmine laughed.

"Well, he might be in trouble again this year," said Ellie seriously. "The riddle says that Queen Malice's second thunderbolt is hidden in Unicorn Valley."

"Oh no!" exclaimed Trixi. "Let's see if we can spot it." She flew over the map and hovered over Unicorn Valley.

They looked down into an orchard full of fruit trees, neat gardens, a steep hill surrounded by multicolored grass, and beautiful emerald-green fields.

"Unicorn Valley is one of the loveliest spots in the kingdom," said Trixi. "Just the sort of place Queen Malice would try to wreck!"

"Well, we won't let her," said Ellie firmly.

"Let's go!" said Jasmine.

Trixi gave the Magic Box a tap with her ring. Then she chanted:

"The evil queen has trouble planned.
Brave helpers fly to save our land!"

Trixi's words appeared on the mirrored lid before streaming up to the ceiling. They swirled around in a dancing cloud

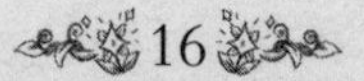

and then surrounded the girls' heads in a glittering, flashing whirlwind.

"We're off to the Secret Kingdom!" cried Jasmine above the sound of rushing air.

The girls grabbed one another's hands as Ellie's bedroom seemed to drop away beneath them. There was a flash of blinding colors . . . and there, spread out below them just as they had been on the map, but much more beautiful, were the rolling green fields of Unicorn Valley.

Fields that were getting closer and closer very quickly!

"Aaarrgh!" shrieked Ellie, screwing her eyes shut. "We're falling!"

Into the Valley

"We're not falling, we're hang gliding!" called Jasmine from nearby.

Ellie realized that something was wrapped around her body, keeping her safe. She looked up and saw a huge red leaf, fluttering delicately above her head in the wind. Vines descended from it, looping safely around her waist.

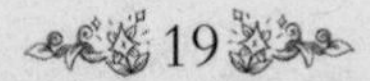

"I think I can see all of Unicorn Valley," called Summer, who was drifting toward Ellie underneath a huge yellow leaf. In the center of the valley was an enormous tree that towered over all the others.

"That's the Great Apple Tree," said Trixi, who was flying along beside them on her own magical leaf. "It was the first tree that ever grew in Unicorn Valley."

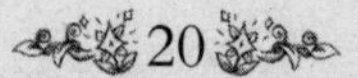

"Um, it's lovely," said Ellie, a bit nervously. "But how do we land?"

"There's a patch of moss just down there," said Trixi. She pointed to a corner of a field filled with flowers. "That will work as a nice soft landing pad. Careful now!"

Flapping their arms and giggling, the girls steered their leaves down to land on the bouncy blue moss. Their leaves settled on top of them with a soft *flump* sound.

"Whew!" said Ellie from under her leaf, which had covered her like a collapsed tent. She pulled it off, but it caught something on her head. Ellie put up her hand to free it and realized she was wearing the beautiful tiara King Merry had given her at the end of their last adventure! She grinned and scrambled about, calling, "Trixi! Are you there?"

"I certainly am," said the little pixie.

Ellie climbed out from under her leaf, and nearly fell over in shock at what she saw. Two white unicorns were galloping gracefully toward them.

Their manes flowed in the wind and their horns sparkled in the sunshine — one silver and one gold. Ellie turned to look in wonder at Summer and Jasmine. Their tiaras had appeared magically on their heads, too, and they were both staring openmouthed at the beautiful creatures.

The bigger unicorn had a lovely wreath of braided leaves and berries resting on her mane. When she reached the girls, she stopped and gently touched the tip of her horn to each of their heads.

"That's a special sign of greeting," Trixi whispered to them. "You should curtsy."

Hastily, Summer and Ellie picked up the edges of their skirts and curtsied clumsily. Jasmine, who was wearing jeans, had to hold out the edges of her top.

"Welcome to Unicorn Valley," said the

unicorn in a regal voice. "I am Silvertail, leader of the unicorns, and this is my daughter, Littlehorn. You are the first humans I have seen in a long time."

The smaller unicorn whinnied. "I've *never* seen a human before," she said. She trotted around the girls, looking at them closely. "You haven't even got tails!" she said in disbelief.

Ellie and Jasmine giggled, but Summer was too awestruck. "I can't believe we're talking to real, live unicorns!" she whispered to Ellie.

Trixi flew her leaf around to hover in front of the girls, and cleared her throat. "Jasmine, Ellie, and Summer are honored guests of King Merry," she explained.

"We know," said Silvertail with a smile. She turned to face the girls. "We can tell from your tiaras that you are Very Important Friends of his. Everyone in the kingdom is talking about how you saved King Merry's birthday party from Queen Malice's nasty thunderbolt!" She shook her mane and harrumphed at the thought of the wicked queen.

"We think that another thunderbolt might have landed here in Unicorn

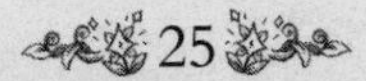

Valley," Ellie told her. "We have to find it before it causes any damage."

Silvertail whinnied anxiously. "My orchard keepers did say that there was something strange near the Great Apple Tree. I was on my way there when you arrived. Perhaps you should come with me?"

"Of course we will," Jasmine agreed.

"It'll be faster if you ride," Silvertail said, looking sideways at the girls' legs. "I will summon my strongest unicorns to carry you."

The three girls exchanged excited glances.

"We're going to ride on unicorns?" cried Jasmine.

Silvertail turned toward the fields and tossed her head. At once, three sturdy unicorns came galloping up. One was a

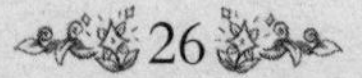

minty green, one was a deep midnight blue, and the last was a charcoal gray. All of them had long, dark manes and tails, and swirly, golden horns. Silvertail introduced them as Fleetfoot, Sleekmane, and Graycoat.

"We'll have a wonderful view from up here," said Jasmine, climbing onto Fleetfoot's mint-green back.

"But we're not too high!" said Ellie, settling onto Graycoat. "Just how I like it!"

"Thank you for carrying us," said Summer to Sleekmane. "This is the first time I've been on a unicorn."

"Hold on tight!" replied Sleekmane with a friendly whinny.

With Trixi hovering beside them, the friends followed Silvertail across Unicorn Valley.

"Have the unicorns always lived here?" asked Ellie.

"No," Silvertail explained. "Unicorn Valley was founded by a unicorn called Snowmane thousands of years ago. Back then, this whole area was covered with poisonous prickles and carnivorous plants. It was the wildest place in the whole kingdom. But then Snowmane touched a thornbush with her horn and turned it into a lovely magic apple tree. The tree spread its beauty out across the land, and all the awful plants disappeared."

Littlehorn swished her tail, cantering between her mother and the unicorns who carried the girls. "We look after the orchards and keep Unicorn Valley a magical place," she neighed happily.

"Those are the stables, where we sleep," said Silvertail, nodding toward a golden building that was set back from the road in a meadow full of flowers. "And up ahead you can see Happyhooves Academy, our school."

"Oh, the baby unicorns are *so* cute!" exclaimed Summer.

The group slowed down to admire the unicorn school, which was a big field divided into lots of open-air classrooms. Riding on their strong unicorn friends, Ellie, Jasmine, and Summer were soon close enough to see a teacher showing some very young unicorns how to write their names. Concentrating hard, they moved their horns through the air and glittery, floating letters appeared in front of them.

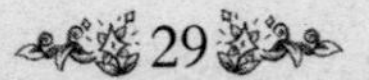

"Those little unicorns have silver horns, like you," said Summer to Littlehorn. "But all the big unicorns have gold horns."

"Our horns stay silver until we're grown up," explained Littlehorn. "Then we take part in the Golden Games and the elders turn our horns golden. You're here just at the right time — the games are this afternoon! I'm competing in the Great Race. The winner gets to be one of the king's royal messengers and carry urgent letters around the kingdom. It's a huge honor!"

"I'm sure that's why the Magic Box has called us now," Jasmine whispered in Ellie's ear. "Queen Malice's thunderbolt is going to wreck the Golden Games!"

"Not if we can help it!" Ellie replied with a grin.

After a short trip, the girls trotted into the orchards, where hundreds of neat trees were being tended by older unicorns.

"This is the Royal Apple Orchard," Silvertail explained, "where all the apples in the Secret Kingdom grow."

"Oh, I wish I had my art supplies so I could draw it!" cried Ellie. "The orchard is

so lovely. . . . Or I could draw the stable. . . . No, the baby unicorns!"

Silvertail smiled. "Come with me just a little farther," she said, "and I will show you the prettiest sight in the whole valley."

Fleetfoot, Sleekmane, and Graycoat cantered between two rows of neat trees and came out in a clearing.

Right in the center was the enormous tree the girls had seen as they glided into the kingdom. It was even bigger close-up.

"Its trunk is as big as my house!" gasped Jasmine.

The unicorns knelt so that Ellie, Summer, and Jasmine could jump down and walk over to the tree. Its ancient branches stretched out above them, heavy with gleaming apples.

"This is the Great Apple Tree that Snowmane created," said Silvertail. "Without it, Unicorn Valley would turn back into a wild and dark place."

"It's amazing!" breathed Ellie.

"This is where the orchard keepers said they saw something strange," said Silvertail. "Maybe the thunderbolt is hidden nearby."

The girls started looking all over the trunk of the tree. Trixi flew her leaf high up into the branches. But they couldn't see any sign of Queen Malice's thunderbolt.

Suddenly there was a whinny of alarm from the other side of the tree. Trixi gave the girls a worried glance, and they all ran around to see what was the matter.

Silvertail was there, staring at something stuck deep in the earth between the roots of the Great Apple Tree. It was a hard black shard that glistened horribly — the tip of Queen Malice's thunderbolt!

"Oh no!" Silvertail neighed urgently.

"Queen Malice's nasty thunderbolt is stuck in the roots of the Great Apple Tree! If the tree is hurt, its magic will disappear, and the whole valley will go back to being a wasteland!"

Slimy Caterpillars and Twisty Vines

The girls started inspecting the tree's lower branches to check for damage.

"I'll check the fruit," Littlehorn said. She concentrated hard, and with a wave of her horn an apple floated down from the top of the tree. It landed on the ground in front of her. Littlehorn nudged it with her horn and then froze.

"What's wrong?" Summer asked. As she watched, a lump rose on the apple's rosy skin. Then it burst — and out came the head of a big, purple, black-spotted caterpillar.

"That's a slime caterpillar!" Trixi cried. "They usually live on the other side of the kingdom, in the grounds of Queen

Malice's horrible Thunder Castle. The more they eat, the bigger they get!"

The funny-looking creature nosed around in the warm air and stuck its tongue out at the girls before burrowing back out of sight.

"Yuck!" gasped Ellie, stepping backward into Littlehorn, who stumbled and knocked over a basketful of apples.

The fruit spilled out onto the ground, and more caterpillars fell out with it.

"Ugh, they're horrible!" said Jasmine, looking at one of the slimy creatures, which was chomping on an apple enthusiastically.

Summer watched a caterpillar as it swallowed a big chunk of apple and then burped loudly. "They're just hungry," she said kindly.

"Summer, you'd love any animal — no matter how disgusting it is!" Ellie teased her friend.

"Let's see if I can get rid of them," said Trixi, guiding her leaf down next to the nearest caterpillar and tapping it with her ring. She chanted:

"You greedy things aren't wanted here.
This spell will make you disappear!"

Nothing happened.

"Queen Malice's magic is too strong for me." Trixi sighed.

The girls exchanged dismayed looks.

"We'll have to destroy the thunderbolt," Silvertail said. "I'll get my strongest unicorns and we'll pull it right out of the ground."

"It's no use," Trixi told her. "In order to get rid of the thunderbolt we'll have to break Queen Malice's spell."

"What will we do if the caterpillars hurt the tree?" Littlehorn asked. She was standing beneath the Great Apple Tree, gazing unhappily at the caterpillars, who were wriggling about among the spilled apples and chomping happily. A big, sparkling teardrop

rolled from one of her eyes. Where it splashed onto the grass, a tiny flower started to grow. "If the valley turns back the way it was, we'll have nowhere to go."

Silvertail looked at her daughter. "Why don't you go and practice for the race, Littlehorn?" she said kindly. "It'll take your mind off things. And you girls could all go and watch," she suggested, turning to Ellie, Summer, and Jasmine. "Maybe you'll be able to find more clues about what Queen Malice is up to, and how to stop her. My orchard keepers are the best gardeners in the Secret Kingdom. I'm sure they can take care of the caterpillars until we find out how to break Malice's spell. I'll stay here to help them."

"And I'll put a holding spell around the tree so that the caterpillars can't

spread to the rest of the orchard," Trixi told them.

"Yes, let's go to the practice area," Summer said to Littlehorn comfortingly, stroking her hand along the unicorn's coat. "We'll probably come up with an idea there."

The little unicorn nodded bravely and led the way out of the apple orchards, toward the racetrack. As they walked into the gardens, the girls looked around them anxiously, trying to spot any other signs of Queen Malice's mischief.

Summer noticed that Littlehorn was looking down at her hooves as she walked, with a worried expression on her face.

"Why don't you tell us about the Golden Games?" Summer asked to distract her.

The little unicorn looked happier at the thought of the afternoon's fun.

"Well, there's the Great Race, of course," she said. "And there are lots of other games and sports, and feats of unicorn magic, too."

"That sounds wonderful." Summer smiled as the girls reached the racetrack. It circled a playing field and a small hill, which was already crowded with unicorns watching the others practice. The track was covered with grass that grew in colored lines to show the runners where to go.

"What game are they playing?" asked Summer, pointing to some unicorns on the big field inside the track, who were leaping up at shining golden hoops that floated magically in the air and catching them on their horns.

"That's Unicorn-Horn Hoopla," said Littlehorn proudly. "And over there, they're playing a game of Runaway Rounders."

The girls watched a team of unicorns who were using their horns to hit a bright red ball. Every time the ball hit the ground it sprouted little legs and tried to run away from the fielders.

"Look, there's King Merry!" said Ellie, pointing excitedly. The little king looked very sharp in his royal robes, except that he had bits of paper sticking out of all his pockets, and ink stains on his cloak.

He was pacing up and down beside the track, scratching his head so hard that his half-moon spectacles were knocked almost off his nose.

"He looks worried," said Trixi. "I'd better see if he's okay."

Summer, Ellie, and Jasmine hurried over to the king, who was muttering to himself absentmindedly.

"Now, let me see," he said. "It is your honor to address me today. . . . Dearie me, no, that's not right. I mean, it is my honor to address you tomorrow. . . . Oh my goodness, no, that won't do either."

"Is he practicing his welcome speech?" Summer whispered to Trixi.

"I think he must be," replied the pixie. "He's not very good at remembering his lines!"

The king stopped pacing and patted his pockets as if he was looking for something. Trixi flew forward and conjured up a large spotted hanky, magicking his robes clean and tidy at the same time.

"Hello!" King Merry said cheerfully. "Girls, how nice to see you again. Are you here for the games?"

"Not quite," Ellie explained. "The Magic Box has brought us here. There's a thunderbolt in the roots of the Great Apple Tree."

"And it's already causing trouble," said Jasmine. "There are horrible slime caterpillars attacking the tree."

"How terrible!" said the king. "Do you have a plan to get rid of the thunderbolt?" He looked at the girls hopefully.

"Not yet," Ellie admitted. "But we're working on it."

"Wow, look at her go!" Summer said, pointing at Littlehorn, who was now racing around the colored track with five other young unicorns. "She's so fast!"

In spite of her worries, Summer couldn't help smiling as the beautiful creatures galloped along, urging one another on. "We won't let the unicorns down," she promised King Merry.

But just as the words left her mouth, something dreadful happened!

Right in front of the racing unicorns, a cluster of long green weeds broke

through the surface of the track. The thick stalks immediately began to grow, snaking out across the grass in all directions. The nasty plants slithered out and tangled themselves in the legs of the running unicorns. Four of the runners got so tripped up they fell horn over hoof. Littlehorn only escaped by leaping high into the air as a stalk tried to grab her tail.

"What on earth are those?" cried Ellie as one of the weeds burst up through

the ground at Jasmine's feet. Ellie and Summer grabbed it and pulled as hard as they could, but the wriggling stem slipped out of their hands and kept on growing.

"It must be because of the Great Apple Tree!" Trixi cried. "With the caterpillars eating the fruit, the tree must be getting weaker. And since its magic is fading, the horrible weeds are coming back to Unicorn Valley! Quick, head for the hill!"

Everyone started running up the hill, but new vines began springing up all around them, and they had to dodge the stalks as they ran. The girls and unicorns managed to scramble to the top of the hill quickly, but King Merry lagged behind. He was out of breath, and Trixi had to help push him up the slope. They had almost reached the girls when a weed curled around King Merry's foot and tripped him.

Ellie dashed down to help him, but one of the vines wound around her waist. As Summer and Jasmine watched in horror, the vicious vine started pulling her down the hill!

Storm Sprites!

"Get off my friend!" Jasmine shouted, hitting the stalk that was wound tightly around Ellie.

"Hold on!" Summer called, grabbing Ellie's hands.

Jasmine started tugging at the clinging vine. With both of them working together, the weed's grip soon started to loosen.

"It's working!" exclaimed Ellie. The vine finally lost its grip — and she, Jasmine, and Summer fell over in a big heap on the ground.

"Whew!" Ellie sighed. "That was close!" The girls struggled back to the top of the hill, where Trixi, King Merry, Littlehorn, and the other unicorns were standing.

"The weeds are growing out of control!" exclaimed Jasmine, pointing down the hill, where even more yucky plants were popping up.

"We'll have to cancel the Golden Games." King Merry frowned. "There's no way we can hold them here with all these weeds in the way. Trixi, could you send a glowworm announcement to warn everyone to stay away?"

Trixi tapped her ring, and it began to shine softly. A few moments later, lots of little lights appeared around them as hundreds of glowworms woke up. The girls looked in amazement at the little lights that shone weakly in the daylight.

"There are glowworms across the kingdom," Trixi explained. "They'll pass our message on to everyone who sees them."

Trixi flew over to tell the glowworms the message, but Summer stopped her.

"Oh, please don't call off the games yet," she begged. "If you do, Queen Malice will get her way and all the unicorns will be miserable. Littlehorn and the others won't be able to get their golden horns, and King Merry won't get a new messenger. We have to fix this!"

"But what can we do?" Trixi cried anxiously. "Without the Great Apple Tree's magic, soon the valley will be completely ruined."

"Wait a minute," Ellie said. "We need to work out how we're going to break Queen Malice's thunderbolt. At King Merry's birthday party, we broke the spell by making sure everyone had fun. So if Queen Malice wants to ruin the Golden Games and the Great Race, then we have to make sure that they go ahead."

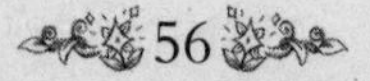

"But how?" Trixi asked. "We'll never clear all these weeds away in time, and we can't have the Great Race without a racetrack."

Summer smiled. "I have an idea! There's always a balance in nature, even if Queen Malice's magic is involved. We've got hungry caterpillars at the Great Apple Tree, and plants that won't stop growing at the racetrack. . . . I think we should take the caterpillars to the Golden Games!"

"The caterpillars won't enjoy the games!" King Merry spluttered. "They're very lazy and they don't like sports."

Ellie smiled as she realized what her friend had in mind. "Not to take part in the games!" She laughed. "If we bring the greedy caterpillars here, they'll eat up all the weeds!"

"They'll chomp the racetrack clean!" agreed Jasmine.

"And then the games can go on!" Summer said, beaming.

Trixi danced excitedly around on her leaf. "I really think it might work, girls," she said. "Thank goodness you're here!"

"But how are we going to get back to the Great Apple Tree?" Jasmine asked, looking down at the weeds that were snaking all over the racetrack. "We're stranded!"

"I can take care of that!" Trixi said cheerfully. "Everyone hold hands — or hooves."

"I'll stay here, Trixi," King Merry announced. "Someone has to stay with the other unicorns and keep them calm."

"He doesn't like being magicked around," Trixi whispered to the girls. "It tangles up his beard and makes him dizzy!"

The girls giggled.

With Ellie, Summer, Jasmine, and Littlehorn all holding on to one another, Trixi cast a spell:

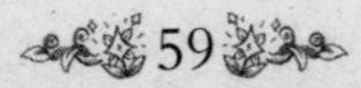

"Help us get where we need to be:
Under the Great Apple Tree!"

Ellie shut her eyes tightly, and when she opened them again they were all standing in the clearing by the tree. She hadn't felt a thing!

"The caterpillars are much bigger now," Summer said.

Trixi's magic spell was keeping the slime caterpillars from spreading, but they were growing quickly as they munched apple after apple and nibbled on the tree trunk.

One of the orchard-keeper unicorns sighed. "And the larger they get, the more they eat!"

"That's a good thing!" Jasmine grinned. "There are lots of horrible weeds growing

at the racetrack, and the caterpillars can help us by eating them all up! We just need to get them there. . . ." Suddenly, she spotted a large apple cart nearby with some fruit in it. "Aha!" she said. "That'll be perfect! If we load that cart full of the tastiest apples, the caterpillars are sure to jump in there, too."

Trixi released her holding spell, and Ellie and Summer set to work heaping armfuls of fruit into the cart. But the caterpillars paid no attention.

"If only we could get them to understand where we want them to go," said Summer thoughtfully.

"How could we do that?" asked Trixi.

Summer thought for a moment longer. "We need a trail of food to lead the caterpillars all the way to the cart."

"That's an excellent idea!" said Trixi, smiling. "I'll do it right away."

The little pixie tapped her ring. It glowed, then something green unfurled from it and fell to the ground. It was a crisp, fresh cabbage leaf.

More leaves appeared from her ring, and Trixi arranged them in a line, leading from the Great Apple Tree into the cart.

One of the caterpillars raised its head, sniffing the air. Then it licked its lips hungrily, crawled forward, and began to nibble at the leaf.

It wasn't long before excited caterpillars were following one another toward the cart. One by one they oozed closer and crawled up into the cart, leaving a slimy trail behind them.

Once all the caterpillars were gathered

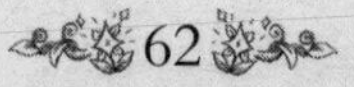

up, the girls packed more apples and berries around them to make sure they had plenty to eat.

When everyone was ready, Trixi tapped her ring once more and the whole group was instantly transported back to the hill.

It was worse than they'd imagined. The racetrack was completely covered with horrible weeds, and King Merry was marooned at the top of the hill next to two sad-looking unicorns.

"We've brought the caterpillars from the Great Apple Tree," Ellie called up to him from the other side of the track. "They'll gobble these vines right up!"

By now, the caterpillars had finished eating the food in the cart. When the girls looked in, there was nothing to be seen except apple cores and enormous, sleepy caterpillars.

"What if they're too full to eat the weeds?" Summer asked anxiously.

But when the slimy creatures spotted the moving weeds, they woke up at once. They licked their lips and crawled toward them eagerly, making funny little gobbling sounds. They quickly began to chomp their way through the mass of twisty green stalks.

"Our plan is working!" Trixi said, clapping her hands delightedly and flying her leaf in a figure eight.

"Good job, Ellie, Summer, and Jasmine!" King Merry called, leading the unicorns down the hill.

"Soon the racetrack will be clear!" said Jasmine as the girls moved the rest of the caterpillars off the carts. "Nothing's going to stop us now!"

Ellie gasped and grabbed her friend's arm. "Uh-oh, something might," she said, pointing behind them. "Look back there."

The girls turned to look. Not far away, two horrid-looking creatures were flying toward the racetrack on top of thunderclouds. Their spiky fingers were outstretched and their dark eyes gleamed with nastiness.

"Queen Malice's Storm Sprites!" said Summer.

The ugly creatures zoomed closer on their thunderclouds. One of them blew a raspberry at the girls.

"Give those caterpillars to us!" the other one shouted. "We're going to spread them everywhere so they eat every single plant, tree, and bush around. Unicorn Valley will become a wasteland, and there's nothing you can do about it!"

A Slimy Surprise

"We can't let the Storm Sprites take the caterpillars!" Summer cried.

Just then, Jasmine noticed something by the entrance to the racetrack — a stand full of juicy-looking blue melons.

"Quick, help me grab some really big caterpillars," Jasmine said. "No time to explain — just trust me."

Ellie and Summer helped Jasmine find three large caterpillars and carry them toward the stall of melons. The caterpillars were so fat now that each girl could lift only one of them, and they were very slimy!

"Whew!" puffed Ellie as she put her heavy caterpillar in place. "I get it, Jasmine. The caterpillars will make the ground slippery, and the Storm Sprites will fall over!"

"Brilliant idea," Trixi said as she flew overhead. "Those are sugar melons. They're so sweet and tasty the caterpillars won't be able to resist them!"

Sure enough, as soon as the caterpillars spotted the yummy-looking sugar melons, they crawled eagerly across the path to get to them, leaving three super-slippery trails behind them.

"Okay, you win," Jasmine called to the sprites. "We'll give you the caterpillars. Here, take these ones."

The sprites laughed nastily, then hopped off their thunderclouds and flew down to the ground, narrowing their black eyes as if they were getting ready to spring.

"Whoa!" shouted the first sprite as he landed. "It's slippery!"

His foot shot out from underneath him and hit the other sprite on the ankle. The second sprite gave a wail, hopped on one leg, then stumbled his way across the road, waving his arms frantically.

The Storm Sprites had landed right in the slippery caterpillar goo!

Neither of them could find a firm place to stand. First they slid into each other, then they tried to grab each other. Finally they both fell down in a tangled heap among the sugar melons.

"You knocked me over, Slug-Breath," one of them shouted.

"No, you tripped me!" the other complained bitterly from underneath a squashed melon.

The girls stood beside the road, giggling at the sight of Queen Malice's henchmen lying surrounded by squashed melons and slime.

The unicorns laughed, too — all except Fleetfoot, Graycoat, and Sleekmane, who were standing over the Storm Sprites, giving them very stern looks.

"You two are coming with us," Graycoat whinnied. "You can help us tidy up the orchard. That should keep you out of trouble until the Golden Games are over."

The unicorns marched the Storm Sprites off toward the orchard, with the sprites still bickering loudly and pushing and shoving each other.

"There won't *be* any games unless the caterpillars have cleared the track," Jasmine said anxiously. But when she looked at the racecourse, there wasn't a weed to be seen! The grass was visible again, and lying sleepily on it, looking fatter than ever, were the slime caterpillars! The one closest to Jasmine

was lying on its back, with its hundreds of feet up in the air, snoring loudly.

Suddenly there was a whinny, and Silvertail came racing up to them from the direction of the Great Apple Tree. “Queen Malice’s thunderbolt has broken!” she told them excitedly. “The tree has already begun to repair itself!”

"We did it!" cried Jasmine.

"We will always be grateful for what you have done today," Silvertail said gravely. "But I am afraid there is still one problem."

The friends exchanged a look.

"The caterpillars!" they all said at once.

What were they going to do with the greedy creatures?

"We have to find somewhere else for them to live," said Trixi.

"Yes," Summer agreed. "We can't send the poor things back to Queen Malice."

But as they watched, the caterpillars started to wriggle. After a few moments, they had coated themselves in silk, which quickly hardened into solid cocoons.

"What's happening?" King Merry

asked. Silvertail knelt down and nudged the nearest cocoon with her horn.

"I don't know," she said, "but at least they won't need feeding for a while!"

Everyone helped move the cocoons carefully into the cart, where they'd be

out of the way of the Golden Games. It was a lot easier now that the caterpillars weren't wiggling around!

"Just in time!" said Silvertail, smiling as Jasmine put the last cocoon carefully into the cart. "We're ready for the opening ceremony. Summer, Ellie, and Jasmine, you must stay and be our guests of honor."

Silvertail led the girls to the best spot on the hill, next to King Merry. Trixi magicked up floating cushions for them all, and they settled down as the young unicorns made the final preparations for the games.

Once everything was ready, King Merry's cushion floated up above the spectators, and he nervously read out his speech.

"It is my address to honor you this year. . . ." he started to say, getting his words hopelessly jumbled up again.

Summer, Ellie, and Jasmine found it difficult not to giggle, but they didn't want to upset the kindly king. They did their best and managed to stay straight-faced until he had finished.

Then they forgot about laughing as the parade of competitors began. Lots of little unicorns strutted confidently around the track. They all had different ribbons, flowers, and grasses woven into their manes and tails.

The girls all cheered as Littlehorn cantered past proudly.

Finally the unicorns lined up in front of the audience and sang the Secret Kingdom's national song:

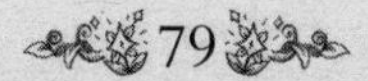

"The Secret Kingdom is a
wonderful land
From frosty mountain to
glittery sand.
Every unicorn, imp, and gnome
Loves our beautiful magical home."

After they'd sung all the verses, the stadium went quiet.

"Look!" Ellie cried, pointing at the sky.

All the little unicorns had raised their heads, and pink and red sparkles were shooting from the tips of their horns like fireworks! The sparkles swirled and twisted into huge letters that twinkled brightly in the evening sky.

"Thank you, Summer,
Ellie, and Jasmine,
for breaking Queen
Malice's spell!"

Summer read out loud.

"Wow!" whispered Jasmine.

Then the letters joined and changed, coming together again to spell out:

Let the Golden
Games begin!

The Golden Games

The girls oohed and aahed in wonder as they saw one amazing event after another. Some of the graceful unicorns took part in a jumping race, leaping over hurdles made of shimmering magic. Others jumped high in the air to catch golden hoops on their horns. There was so much going on that Ellie, Summer, and Jasmine hardly knew where to look first!

The high point of the games was the Great Race. Summer, Ellie, and Jasmine held on to their cushions with excitement as Silvertail fired a burst of sparkles from her horn to start the race and the unicorns sped off.

"Come on, Littlehorn!" chanted the girls.

At first Littlehorn was in the lead! But a larger, red-dappled unicorn was running on the inside lane, and he was gradually overtaking her. . . .

Jasmine stood up and shouted encouragement while Ellie cheered and Summer crossed her fingers and pressed them against her cheeks.

Trixi was so excited she couldn't bear to look, so she hid behind her human friends. "Tell me when it's over!" she said.

Littlehorn put on a burst of speed, creeping closer and closer to the larger unicorn.

"You can do it, Littlehorn!" Jasmine yelled at the top of her lungs. Littlehorn lowered her horn determinedly and galloped as fast as she could. She caught up to the other unicorn — and won by a horn!

Trixi and the girls watched with pride as King Merry crowned Littlehorn with a wreath of glitterberries and officially named her as his new royal messenger.

Finally all the young unicorns climbed up to the top of the hill and were greeted by their family and friends. The celebrations were nearly over, and the girls knew it was almost time for them to go home. Only one last thing remained — to watch Littlehorn and the other young unicorns get their golden horns!

Silvertail whinnied and the unicorns all fell silent. "This is when we perform the coming-of-age ceremony," [illegible]id, "and when we honor those who help us."

Littlehorn suddenly looked very serious. She and the other young unicorns gathered in a circle facing inward and slowly lowered their heads. As their horns touched, there was a tinkling sound, and the air above the circle started to glow. The girls gasped in wonder as the little unicorns' horns slowly changed from a sparkling silver to a glorious golden color. As soon as the change was complete there was a great roar of noise as all the unicorns neighed and stomped their hooves in celebration. Littlehorn grinned widely, going cross-eyed in her attempts to look at her newly golden horn.

The noise died down as Silvertail moved into the middle of the circle. She gave a long whinny, and all of the unicorns pointed their horns to one spot in the air. Bursts of sparkly magic streamed out of their horns, coming together to form

a glittery shape. Slowly the shape came into focus — it was a tiny silver unicorn horn! When it was complete, Silvertail whinnied again and the horn floated over to the girls.

"This is a gift to thank you for saving Unicorn Valley from Queen Malice's

meanness. Without you, our beautiful home would have been destroyed. We will always be grateful," said Silvertail, bowing to the girls. Behind her, the unicorns bowed their heads. Even Trixi, with a huge smile on her little face, dipped a little curtsy.

Summer realized all the unicorns were waiting for them to take the gift. She stepped forward nervously and carefully grasped the sparkling horn. It was no longer than her little finger, and seemed to weigh almost nothing. It was covered with a beautiful spiral pattern, just like Littlehorn's.

Just then there was a gasp from the crowd. The girls turned and peered down at the apple carts. The caterpillar cocoons were moving and shaking. All of a sudden, one of them popped open and a gorgeous butterfly with shimmering purple patterns on its wings flew up into the air! The cocoons were hatching! Soon, another butterfly appeared, and then another, until the air was filled with them, dancing and fluttering about on their new wings.

"They're beautiful!" Summer exclaimed.

"Who'd have thought those slimy caterpillars could become such gorgeous butterflies." Jasmine smiled.

"I hope they won't be quite as hungry now that they're grown-up," Ellie said.

Everyone admired the beautiful butterflies as they flitted and fluttered above, oohing and aahing at their dance in the sky.

After a few minutes, Silvertail hushed the crowd. "We will be silent for a moment," she said seriously. "Now, Summer, listen carefully."

Summer did so, wondering what was supposed to happen.

Then she gasped. Among the flapping of their wings, she could suddenly hear the butterflies calling out.

"Thank you!" they all cried. "We didn't mean to cause any trouble."

"I can understand the butterflies!" she said in amazement.

Ellie and Jasmine listened hard. "I can't hear anything," Ellie said.

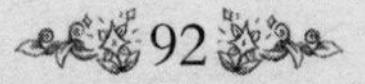

"The silver horn gives you the ability to talk to and understand all animals," said Trixi, smiling.

Summer handed the horn to her friends so that they could hear the little voices.

Trixi tapped her ring and a sparkly spell in the shape of a butterfly appeared and flew away, leaving a glittery trail. "This will lead you to Flower Forest," she told the beautiful butterflies.

As the butterflies started to follow Trixi's spell to their new home,

Silvertail turned to the girls solemnly. "You are now honorary members of our unicorn family. You are Summer Kindhoof. You are Ellie Flamemane. And you are Jasmine Braveheart," she said as she gently touched each of the girls in turn with her horn. "Should you ever need us, we will be there to help you."

The girls looked at one another in amazement. "Thank you," Jasmine managed to say.

Smiling happily, the girls said good-bye to the unicorns. Trixi kissed each girl on the nose, then hovered above their heads and conjured up the magic whirlwind that would take them back home.

"See you soon!" was the last thing they heard as they were lifted higher and higher above beautiful Unicorn Valley.

Then, with a flash of light, they found themselves settling softly onto Ellie's rug.

Ordinary daylight filled the bedroom, and glinted off the Magic Box, which was sitting on the rug between them.

"Oh, wow," said Ellie, looking down at the little horn in her hand. "What an amazing adventure."

"I'm so glad we met the unicorns," said Summer.

"But it's a shame that time doesn't pass while we're in the Secret Kingdom," sighed Jasmine. "After all that, I'm hungrier than ever — and the cookies *still* aren't ready!"

Ellie and Summer laughed.

Suddenly the Magic Box began to glow, and its lid slowly opened. Ellie gently placed the silver horn into one of the

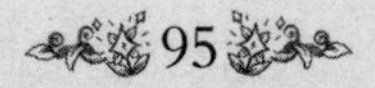

compartments inside. "I hope we can go back to the Secret Kingdom soon," she said.

"You can count on that, Flamemane," said Jasmine with a chuckle. "We still have to find four more of those nasty thunderbolts. I wonder where we'll go next. How about the Wandering

Waterfalls? Ooh, or the Mystic Meadows? King Merry said the pixies have toadstool fights there!"

"I'd love to see both of those places." Summer sighed. "But the important thing is to be there for Trixi and King Merry, and to save the kingdom from Queen Malice!"

"That's for certain," agreed Jasmine, grinning. "All right — race you to the cookies!"

Laughing, the three friends ran downstairs.

In the next Secret Kingdom adventure, Ellie, Summer, and Jasmine visit

Cloud Island!

Read on for a sneak peek. . . .

A Message from the Secret Kingdom

"I wish we didn't have so much homework to do." Ellie Macdonald sighed as she walked home from school with her friends. "I've got to write a story for English, and I don't know where to start!"

"Let's all do our homework together at my house," suggested Jasmine Smith. "We can put some music on and help one another."

"Great idea," agreed Summer Hammond, linking arms with Jasmine and Ellie. "Even homework can be fun when you do it with friends."

"I wouldn't go that far." Ellie grinned, her green eyes twinkling. "But it's better than doing it on your own."

Laughing, they all made their way to Jasmine's house and hurried into the kitchen.

A big bag of chocolate cookies and a note were sitting on the kitchen table. Jasmine picked up the note and read it out loud:

"Hi, Jasmine,
I'm sure you've brought Ellie
and Summer back with you,
so share these with them! There's some
homemade lemonade in the fridge as well.

See you at five.

Mom."

"Your mom's so nice!" said Summer.

Jasmine smiled. "I wonder what made her think you'd be with me."

"Yeah, you would think we spent all our time together," joked Ellie.

Summer giggled. She, Jasmine, and Ellie all lived in a little town called Honeyvale and went to the same school. They had been best friends since they were little, and they went over to one another's houses so much that they all felt like home!

Jasmine opened the fridge and took out a big jug of lemonade while Summer grabbed three glasses and a plate.

"Now, let's deal with our homework," said Jasmine, putting everything on a tray and leading the way upstairs. "Then we can start having some real fun."

"Hey, you've got the Magic Box on your dressing table!" exclaimed Ellie as they all spilled into Jasmine's bedroom, which was quite small, but beautifully decorated. The walls were a gorgeous hot-pink color, and red floaty netting hung down over the bed.

"I didn't want to miss a message from the Secret Kingdom!" Jasmine said.

They all looked at the beautiful wooden box. It was covered with intricate carvings of fairies and unicorns and had a mirrored lid studded with green stones. It looked like a jewelry box, but it was *much* more than that.

"I slept with it under my pillow last time I was taking care of it!" Ellie laughed.

The girls had found the Magic Box at a school rummage sale, when it had mysteriously appeared in front of them. It belonged to King Merry, the ruler of the Secret Kingdom.

The Secret Kingdom was a magical world that no one knew existed — no one except Jasmine, Summer, and Ellie! It was a beautiful crescent moon–shaped island, where mermaids, unicorns, pixies, and elves all lived happily together.

But the kingdom was in terrible trouble. Queen Malice, the king's horrible sister, was so angry that the people of the Secret Kingdom had chosen King Merry to be their ruler instead of her that she had sent six horrible thunderbolts into the kingdom to cause all kinds of trouble. Summer, Jasmine, and Ellie had already found two of the thunderbolts and broken their nasty spells.

"I wish we could go on another magical adventure." Ellie sighed.

"Me too," agreed Jasmine, taking her books out of her backpack and sprawling out on the carpet. She tucked her long dark hair behind her ears. "Come on, let's get this over with," she said, reaching for a chocolate cookie.

Ellie got her English book out and started chewing on her pencil. She was looking around the room, trying to come up with an idea for her story, when something caught her eye. "I don't think we'll be doing homework after all!" she cried in delight. "The Magic Box is glowing!"

The girls all jumped up to look. They crowded around the box, watching excitedly as, letter by letter, words started to form in the magic mirror.

"I wonder what mischief Queen Malice is up to now," said Jasmine, shuddering at the thought of the horrid queen and her wicked plans to make everyone in the kingdom as miserable as she was.

"We'll have to solve the riddle to find out," said Summer as she studied the words in the mirror. Then she slowly read them out loud:

"A thunderbolt there will be found
Way up high above the ground.
A white and fluffy floating land
Needs you all to lend a hand!"

Jasmine quickly wrote the riddle down before the words disappeared into the mirror. "What does it mean?" she asked.

Ellie looked puzzled. "A floating land — it must be an island."

"Let's check the map," said Jasmine. "We might be able to spot it."

As if it had heard them, the Magic Box opened up, revealing the six compartments inside. Only two of the spaces were filled, one by a map of the Secret Kingdom that King Merry had given them after their first visit, and the other by a little silver unicorn horn. It was small, but it had enormous power — whoever held it could talk to animals!

Summer took out the map carefully and spread it out gently on Jasmine's floor.

The three girls sat around it, their heads touching as they peered at it excitedly. There were a few small islands in Mermaid Reef, and a couple more off the shore of Glitter Beach. They all moved magically on the map as the aquamarine sea bobbed up and down, but none of them looked white or fluffy.

"It's not here!" Summer said anxiously.

"But it has to be!" cried Ellie. "We have to solve the riddle so we can get to the Secret Kingdom and find the thunderbolt before something horrible happens!"

Jasmine stood and started pacing up and down the middle of her room with a worried expression on her face.

"Let's read the riddle again," Summer suggested. "We have to be missing something. 'A white and fluffy floating land.' Well, these islands aren't white or fluffy."

"'Way up high above the ground . . .'" Jasmine muttered to herself. Then she glanced down at the map and laughed. Summer and Ellie were still searching the bottom of the map, looking at every inch of sea. But Jasmine had realized something. "We shouldn't be looking in the sea!" she cried. "We should be looking in the sky!"

"Of course!" said Ellie with a grin. "What's white and fluffy and floats?"

"A cloud!" exclaimed Summer.

"And here's Cloud Island!" Ellie exclaimed, pointing to a puffy white cloud at the top of the map. "That must be it. Let's summon Trixi!"

The girls put their hands on the Magic Box, pressing their fingers against the green stones on its carved wooden lid.

"The answer is Cloud Island," Jasmine whispered.

Suddenly there was a flash of light, followed by a squeal. Trixibelle had appeared, but the little pixie was trapped among the netting over Jasmine's bed!

"Keep still!" Jasmine cried as the little pixie twisted around. She was trying to free herself, but was only getting more and more caught up.

"I'm trying!" Trixi cried, giving a yelp as she tumbled off her leaf.

Ellie, Jasmine, and Summer quickly climbed up onto Jasmine's bed to untangle Trixi from the mesh. Ellie's nimble fingers carefully unwrapped the netting from Trixi's flower hat, while Jasmine and Summer helped Trixi pull her arms and legs free.

"There!" Ellie said as she untangled the last bit.

"Whew!" Trixi sighed, jumping back on her leaf and flying in a quick twirl before straightening out her skirt and the flower hat that covered her messy blond hair. "Hello, girls," she exclaimed, flying over to kiss them all on the tips of their noses. She landed on the edge of Jasmine's bedside table. "It's lovely to see you all again. Have you figured out where the next thunderbolt is?"

"We think it's somewhere called Cloud Island," Summer said.

Trixi nodded. "There's no time to waste! We need to go to the kingdom right away."

The girls all looked excitedly at one another. They were off on another magical adventure — this time to an island in the sky!

As the girls watched, Trixi tapped the Magic Box with her ring and chanted a spell:

"The evil queen has trouble planned.
Brave helpers fly to save our land."

Her words appeared on the mirrored lid and then soared toward the ceiling, separated into sparkles, and tumbled down again in a colorful burst, whizzing around the girls' heads until they formed a whirlwind. The rushing air picked the girls up, and moments later Ellie, Summer, and Jasmine were dropped onto something springy. It was the softest landing ever!

Summer looked around in astonishment. It felt like she was on a huge bouncy bed, but all she could see around her was white. Hesitantly, she put out her hand to touch the fluffy stuff, and then grinned as she realized — she was standing on a cloud!

Read

Cloud Island

to find out what
happens next!

Be in on the secret.
Collect them all!

Enjoy six sparkling adventures.

Secret Kingdom
Cloud Island
ROSIE BANKS
SCHOLASTIC
Secret Kingdom
Mermaid Reef
ROSIE BANKS
SCHOLASTIC
Secret Kingdom
Magic Mountain
ROSIE BANKS
SCHOLASTIC
Secret Kingdom
Glitter Beach
ROSIE BANKS
SCHOLASTIC

Character Profile:
Summer
Hammond

Personality:

Quiet, thoughtful, and caring. If someone's upset, Summer will be the one to notice and help them.

Favorite Color:

Yellow.

Loves:

Animals and reading.

Favorite Place in the Secret Kingdom:

Unicorn Valley. The baby unicorns are so cute!

Family:

Summer has one older brother, Phoenix, and two younger brothers, Finn and Connor. They all live with their mother and stepfather.

Caterpillar Maze

Jasmine, Ellie, and Summer need to get the slime caterpillars to the racetrack. Can you help them find their way through the maze? Watch out for Storm Sprites!

RAINBOW magic™

Which Magical Fairies Have You Met?

- ☑ The Rainbow Fairies
- ☑ The Weather Fairies
- ☑ The Jewel Fairies
- ☑ The Pet Fairies
- ☑ The Dance Fairies
- ☑ The Music Fairies
- ☑ The Sports Fairies
- ☑ The Party Fairies
- ☑ The Ocean Fairies
- ☑ The Night Fairies
- ☑ The Magical Animal Fairies
- ☑ The Princess Fairies
- ☑ The Superstar Fairies
- ☑ The Fashion Fairies
- ☑ The Sugar & Spice Fairies

Find all of your favorite fairy friends at
scholastic.com/rainbowmagic

RAINBOW magic™

SPECIAL EDITION

Which Magical Fairies Have You Met?

3 stories in each one!

- ☐ Joy the Summer Vacation Fairy
- ☐ Holly the Christmas Fairy
- ☐ Kylie the Carnival Fairy
- ☐ Stella the Star Fairy
- ☐ Shannon the Ocean Fairy
- ☐ Trixie the Halloween Fairy
- ☐ Gabriella the Snow Kingdom Fairy
- ☐ Juliet the Valentine Fairy
- ☐ Mia the Bridesmaid Fairy
- ☐ Flora the Dress-Up Fairy
- ☐ Paige the Christmas Play Fairy
- ☐ Emma the Easter Fairy
- ☐ Cara the Camp Fairy
- ☐ Destiny the Rock Star Fairy
- ☐ Belle the Birthday Fairy
- ☐ Olympia the Games Fairy
- ☐ Selena the Sleepover Fairy
- ☐ Cheryl the Christmas Tree Fairy
- ☐ Florence the Friendship Fairy
- ☐ Lindsay the Luck Fairy
- ☐ Brianna the Tooth Fairy
- ☐ Autumn the Falling Leaves Fairy
- ☐ Keira the Movie Star Fairy
- ☐ Addison the April Fool's Day Fairy

SCHOLASTIC

Find all of your favorite fairy friends at
scholastic.com/rainbowmagic

RMSPECIAL12

These are no ordinary princesses—
they're Rescue Princesses!